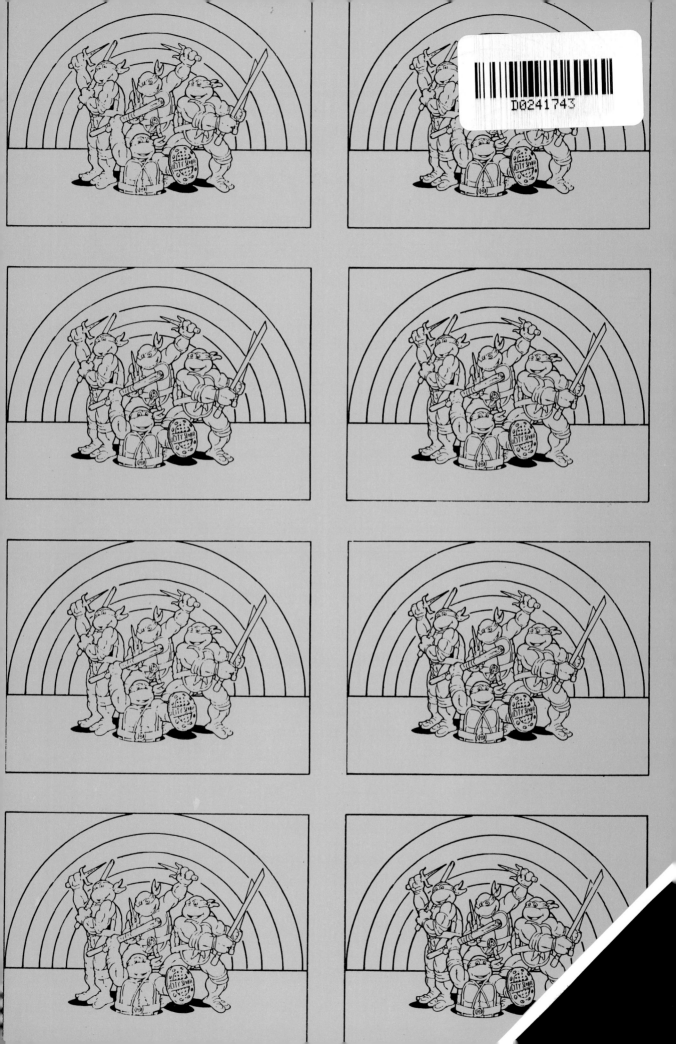

To Richard
from Gran Dawson.

©1990. Mirage Studios.
Licensed by Copyright Promotions Limited.

Text by Angus Allen, illustrations by C.L.I.C. Publishing.

Published by

GRANDREAMS LIMITED
Jadwin House, 205/211 Kentish Town Road, London, NW5 2JU.

Printed in Belgium.

ISBN 0 86227 779 5

# CONTENTS

MICHAELANGELO

DONATELLO

# INVASION OF THE PUNK FROGS

"At last, I have dreamed up the master plan to rid myself, once and for all, of those accursed Turtles!" As his two pea-brained musclemutants, Rock Steady and Bebop, watched, the evil Shredder spoke rapidly into the communicator. He was in touch with Krang, the boss-brain creature of Dimension X...

"And what do you want of me?"

"Mutogen," replied Shredder. "A further supply of the potion that creates mutants. It is my intention to make *more* of them, so that the Turtles will be hopelessly outnumbered!"

"An excellent idea - for once," snapped Krang. "But Mutogen is very *rare* and expensive. And besides, my Technodrome is at present being bombarded by an Ion

storm. It may interfere with the inter-dimensional portal!"

Shredder hated begging. Especially from Krang. But he did so, and at last the sinister brain agreed to attempt the transfer of the Mutogen canister from Dimension X to the normal world.

Unluckily for the arch-criminals, Krang's fears proved true. The Ion storm did interfere with the portal, and instead of dropping to New York, the Mutogen canister landed in the Okefenoke Swamp, in Florida! More than that - it burst open as it hit the water, and almost instantly, it affected four of the ordinary frogs who lived there. As they mutated to human size, their appearance drove a party of *real* human tourists to shriek with alarm and beat a hasty retreat in their camper wagon!

When Krang came through on the communicator to tell him the bad news, Shredder was beside himself with anger. But only for a moment. "Very well," he muttered. "I shall go to Florida to recover the canister." He didn't know it had been broken!

"Wow-*weee*!" Rock Steady clapped his hands. "I'll go pack my surfboard!"

"I'm going alone," barked Shredder.

"Dressed like *that*?" Even Bebop's dim brain could understand that Shredder would stand out like a sore thumb.

"This hologram will disguise me," sneered Shredder. And a device in his hand transformed his appearance into that of a normal man. "Now. You two remain here, and continue to make things hot for those confounded Turtles. Understand?"

"You bet, boss! Yuh huh huh! We'll *like* that!"

In her office at Channel Six Television, April, the Turtles' friend, was once again fielding awkward questions from her scatty assistant, Irma. "Yes, Irma, I do know the Turtles. Happy?"

"No," wailed Irma. "You know them - but I don't! And hey, what's wrong now?" April had turned to her computer, and she had ripped off a print-out that seemed to have filled her with sudden alarm. "Er - you'll have to excuse me, Irma," stammered April. "I've - uh - gotta make tracks..."

She made straight for the sewers where the Turtles hung out with Master Splinter. "Hey, you guys," she said. "Take a look at this! Giant frogs have been reported down in the Florida swamps!"

"Far out," breathed Michaelangelo. "Could they be mutants like us?"

Thoughtfully, Splinter rubbed his chin. "Hmm. Perhaps we should investigate."

"You mean go to Florida?" Michaelangelo's eyes lit up. "The surfing there is *totally* coolamundo!"

"Oh, oh," said Leonardo. "The time may not be right." He was watching the TV screen, and on it, there was an urgent newsflash! "Two vandals are busy trying to smash up Times Square," said the announcer. "One in a Rhinoceros mask, the other in a Wart Hog outfit!"

"Rock Steady and Bebop!" breathed Donatello. "What's sent *them* on the rampage?"

"Perhaps they passed a mirror and saw what they looked like," suggested Raphael.

"Well, we'd better do something about it," said Leonardo. "C'mon, guys!"

April followed them out. She wasn't about to miss the chance of a good story!

11

In the meantime, Shredder had reached Florida. He located the canister, thanks to Krang's co-ordinates, cursed when he found it had leaked all its contents, but within moments, he came upon the frogs, and put two and two together. "If you're mutants," he said, "you should be able to talk."

"Sure we can talk," said one of the frogs.

"Good. Then just remember - I am the friend of all living creatures," said Shredder. "And I hereby recruit you to help me against the evil ones known as - the Turtles!"

"We're game," said the frogs, leaping into Shredder's boat and almost upsetting it. "Lead on!"

Shredder produced a device and triggered it, bathing the frogs in a strange glow. Immediately, they found themselves dressed. "Oh, boy! Clothes. He's tellin' the truth. He really *is* a nice person!"

In Times Square, Rock Steady and Bebop were having the time of their lives. They ripped up fire hydrants, parking meters - anything they could break - and began smashing up everything in sight. "Duhhh - *this'll* draw those green freaks," said Bebop.

"You're right, Bebop," chuckled Rock Steady. "An' here they *are*! Woweee - it's Turtle-trashin' time!"

Donatello was first into the fray. Using his stick, he vaulted straight at Bebop, feet first. But the huge mutant never even shuddered, and Donatello found himself bounced backwards to land in a litter bin. "Phwee-ewww, guys! This is gonna call for something *else*," he gasped.

But at that moment, just as Rock Steady was about to come blasting in with a heavy section of lamppost, the thug's communicator buzzed urgently, and he paused to flip on a picture of Shredder.

"Back to base," ordered the evil one. "Immediately. I found what I wanted, and I need you there!"

"But, boss, we're about to have us some real *fun*," wailed Rock Steady.

"It's an order, you hapless cretin," snarled Shredder. "Move it. *Now!*"

"C'mon, Bebop. Party time's over," groaned Rock Steady. And the villainous pair shot off, leaving the Turtles standing.

"Frogs???" Rock Steady and Bebop could hardly believe their eyes when they joined Shredder and saw the new recruits.

"Yes, frogs, you idiots," barked Shredder. "And just as Splinter has trained the Turtles, *I* have trained *them*. What is more, I have renamed them after *my* historical favourites. Meet Attila the Frog, Genghis Frog, Rasputin the mad Frog, and Napoleon Bonafrog!"

"B-but they're wimps," said Bebop. "The Turtles will mop up the floor with 'em!"

"Show him, Napoleon," smiled Shredder.

"Whatever you say, master!" Bonafrog uncoiled the long whip with which Shredder had armed him, cracked it through the air and caught Rock Steady round the neck. Then, one smart tug, and the bully-boy spun like a top until he fell dizzily to the ground! "Point taken," smirked Bebop. "They might work out, at that!"

In the sewers, Splinter was getting anxious. "We haven't heard anything about Shredder for quite a while," he mused.

"Zilch. Naughtamundo," said Michaelangelo.

"That means, nothing," explained Raphael.

"Don't speak too soon," cried April. "Just take a look at what's come up on the television news!"

Appalled, they all watched as a newscaster told viewers that one of the city's largest banks had been robbed - "by a bunch of green creatures like giant turtles!"

"Turtles?" Donatello shot to his feet. "Guys! We've been framed!"

"And Shredder just has to be at the back of it," said Splinter.

Now there came an interview on screen with the Mayor. "I'm not standing for terrorisation of this city," he said. "I've organised a special anit-Turtle squad to deal with it, and Captain Hoffman here

will be in charge of it." The Mayor introduced a big, mean, hard looking police officer who looked like he ate barbed-wire for breakfast. "You can leave 'em to me, your honour," said Hoffman. "*I'll* stop these criminals!"

In his HQ, Shredder congratulated the frogs. "Well done. Your first mission at the bank went swimmingly."

"Swimmin' is what we do best," said Genghis, blushing with pride. "Are we ready to take over the whole city now?"

"Not quite," replied Shredder. "We need more help." He got through to Krang, who was, as usual, furious at being disturbed. "What is it nowww?" complained Krang.

"More Mutogen," rasped Shredder. "I need it."

"There is no more," said Krang. "But I shall give you the recipe to make it - if you can find the ingredients. Now listen, carefully..."

As Shredder copied down the

details, the Turtles were out looking for him. It was no easy task, especially since they'd been framed and were wanted for bank robbery! At every turn, they seemed to run into the police, and soon they were being chased headlong all over the city. It was pure chance that took them to the Mallory Chemical Works - the very place Shredder had sent the frogs to steal the chemicals he needed to make Mutogen. Genghis Frog broke in with his axe and quickly found exactly what was wanted. "Dexonine and - uh - Phlogiston. We got it!"

"And you'll get *more*!" It was Leonardo's voice, and Turtles and frogs came face to face for the first time. All drew their weapons, but Rasputin Frog was fastest off the mark. His bow shot an explosive arrow into the ceiling, and it burst in a dazzling display of brilliant white light that blinded the Turtles. By the time they got their vision back, the frogs had fled.

"With me, you guys," barked Leonardo. "We can't let 'em get away!"

"Turtlebummer," groaned Michaelangelo as they got outside. "They already *got* away!"

"We have real trouble," said Donatello. "Those chemicals they stole were components of the Mutogen Shredder used to create Rock Steady and Bebop. He's obviously out to make more!"

"Then we're sunk," said Raphael.

"Not quite," said Donatello. "He still needs a third ingredient called Niotrinoline. It's extremely rare." Immediately, Leonardo got onto April in her office. "Hi, April. We need you to check the database and find out where there's a supply of Niotrinoline!"

April punched the buttons of her computer keyboard. "I've got it, she yelled. "A shipment of the stuff is just about to arrive by armoured truck at the Argus Chemical Supply Warehouse!"

15

In his lair, Shredder was carefully mixing the chemicals that the frogs had brought, while Krang gave the instructions over the communications link. "And now," said Krang, "all you need is some Niotrinoline..."

"You never said anything about that," raved Shredder.

"No, I thought I'd keep it as a surprise to make sure you're on your toes," sneered Krang.

Shredder gulped. "You are - unspeakably cruel, Krang!"

"Why, *thaaank* you," smirked the brain. "Now get this. A shipment is due at the Argus Warehouse..."

Now it all began to happen. April, sent by her TV station to interview Captain Hoffman and the city's anti-Turtle squad, saw him climb into the big icer-gun tank he'd been given. He held up a device. "This tunes in to the Turtles' biorhythms," he snarled. "Wherever they are, I'll find them!"

At the same time, the Turtle Blimp was overflying the city and Raphael had spotted the armoured vehicle heading for the Argus Chemical Warehouse.

Then, as the Turtles watched, the frogs pounced from cover, blasting a great hole in the road ahead of the vehicle, to ambush it. "C'mon, Turtles! Let's go! *Turrrrrtle Powerrrrr!*" The control pod detached itself from the blimp and landed at the scene. "Give up, you guys, otherwise it'll be sautee of frogs' legs for dinner."

The frogs gaped - but before either side had time to do a thing, Captain Hoffman's tank screamed round a corner, and its gun traversed. Frogs? Turtles? He couldn't tell the difference - and he picked the frogs to start on! One blast of the gun froze all four of them in neat triangles of pure ice.

"Don't look now, Dudes," shrieked Michaelangelo. "It's our turn now. We're about to be flash-frozen!"

"Not if *I* can help it," yelled Donatello, and he flung one of his daggers straight at the tank. Its amazing power took the muzzle of the ice-gun and thrust it upwards, so that the shot hit a building above and behind. The entire facade was instantly coated with ice...ice that

fell off in chunks as soon as it appeared, and swamped the tank itself! Inside, Hoffman nearly bust a blood-vessel in his fury, trying to get out against the pressure on the hatch.

"Time to make Turtle-tracks," yelled Donatello. But Leonardo stopped them. "We've got to take the frogs with us!"

"Maybe you haven't been keeping up with current events, Dude, but they aren't exactly on our side," said Michaelangelo.

"Nevertheless, they are mutants like us," said Leonardo. "Think what we've been taught by Master Splinter. Maybe we can talk to them once they're unfrozen..."

So it was that they got clear in the nick of time, and took the frogs back to the sewers. Set free, the frogs began by wanting to fight - but Master Splinter stopped the conflict. "There will be no violence," he said.

"Gee, I'm so confused," said Genghis Frog. "We'd been told you fellers were *evil*..."

Patiently, Splinter explained, and in no time at all, the frogs realised how they'd been duped by Shredder.

"So what happens now?" said Attila.

"I have an idea where we can work together against Shredder," grinned Leonardo. "Just listen to me for a while..."

The frogs went back to Shredder, humbly apologetic for losing the vital Niotrinoline. He was livid, but Genghis Frog said that he'd overheard the Turtles saying that they were going to hide the chemical in the old, disused island prison called Stonewall.

Rock Steady and Bebop liked that. They'd both done time in the prison when it was open, and they looked on it as a home from home.

But, when Shredder, his two thick-head heavies, and the frogs made their way to the island and broke in to the old jail, they found the Turtles waiting for them.

"You treacherous frogs," screamed Shredder. "You set me up!"

There would have been a battle royal, but at that moment, Captain Hoffman's anti-Turtle squad helicopter, guided by his device, landed on the roof.

"Yah hah harrr," gloated Shredder. "We'll leave you to face the music, Turtles. While *we* escape!" He pulled out his hologram device and changed himself and his two dumb sidekicks into replicas of Hoffman's police.

Turtles and frogs raced through the corridors, pursued by Hoffman and his goons. They used their projectile guns to lay down a barrage of anti-mutant gas, and now Leonardo and his friends found their senses were reeling. Desperately, they fought to stay ahead.

"We - we've got to get into the - the sewers that - that connect to the mainland," gasped Leonardo.

"This - this is a laundry room," wheezed Raphael. "There must be soakways beneath the floor!"

Michaelangelo rubbed his streaming eyes. "Hey - Dudes! What - what about those exploding arrows that - uh - Rasputin has?"

Rasputin Frog needed no second bidding. "Yeah! I got me the answer," he choked. "Watch me!"

With his last reserves of energy, Rasputin drew back the bowstring and let fly. There came a massive blast of destructive power, and the floor fell in. Next instant, Turtles and frogs were down and away, leaving the prison and the gas and the anti-Turtle squad far behind.

"The Mayor's not gonna like this," grated Hoffman, hurling his Turtle-seeking device to the ground in a fit of fury!

Splinter welcomed them all as they returned to safety. He gave the frogs clear instructions for getting back to their home in Florida. "Life's much better down there," said Genghis. "The big city don't suit us too well!"

"Thanks for coming over to the right side, guys," said Donatello.

"Thanks for showing us which *was* the right side," laughed Napoleon Bonafrog.

In came Michaelangelo, bearing a steaming pizza. "Wait a moment, Dudes," he said. "Before you go, let's eat!"

"Pizza?" said Rasputin. "*Pizza?* Yecch!"

"Thanks, but *no* thanks," said Attila.

The frogs left.

Michaelangelo looked down at the dish in his hands, then up at the others. He shook his head, mystified. "They don't like *pizza? Some* mutants are just plain *weird...*"

# WORD SEARCH 1

Can you find the following 11 characters associated with
the Turtles in the grid below? They can be spelt backwards,
forwards, up, down or diagonally.
Answers on pages 60-61.

LEONARDO
RAPHAEL
SPLINTER
DONATELLO
MICHAELANGELO

APRIL O'NEILL
BEBOP
SHREDDER
ROCKSTEADY
BAXTER STOCKMAN
KRANG

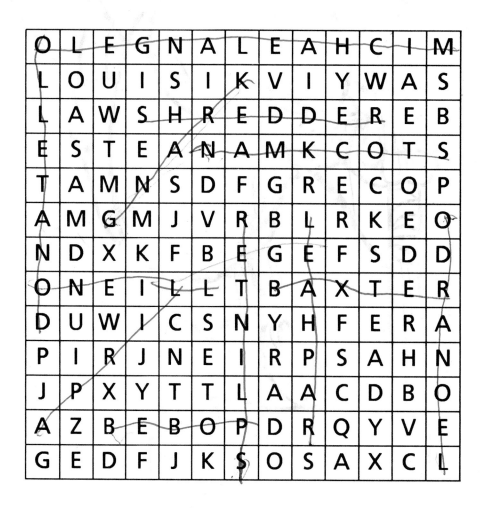

| O | L | E | G | N | A | L | E | A | H | C | I | M |
|---|---|---|---|---|---|---|---|---|---|---|---|---|
| L | O | U | I | S | I | K | V | I | Y | W | A | S |
| L | A | W | S | H | R | E | D | D | E | R | E | B |
| E | S | T | E | A | N | A | M | K | C | O | T | S |
| T | A | M | N | S | D | F | G | R | E | C | O | P |
| A | M | G | M | J | V | R | B | L | R | K | E | O |
| N | D | X | K | F | B | E | G | E | F | S | D | D |
| O | N | E | I | L | L | T | B | A | X | T | E | R |
| D | U | W | I | C | S | N | Y | H | F | E | R | A |
| P | I | R | J | N | E | I | R | P | S | A | H | N |
| J | P | X | Y | T | T | L | A | A | C | D | B | O |
| A | Z | B | E | B | O | P | D | R | Q | Y | V | E |
| G | E | D | F | J | K | S | O | S | A | X | C | L |

RAPHAEL

LEONARDO

# SPOT THE DIFFERENCE

There are 10 differences between the pictures above!
How many can you spot? Answers on pages 60-61.

# COPY AND COLOUR

Copy the picture above in the space below using the
grid as a guide. Then colour in both pictures.

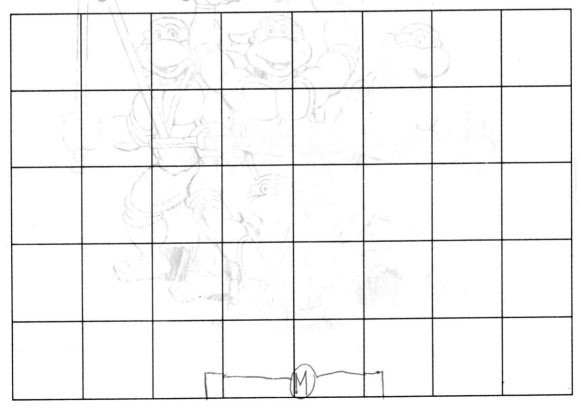

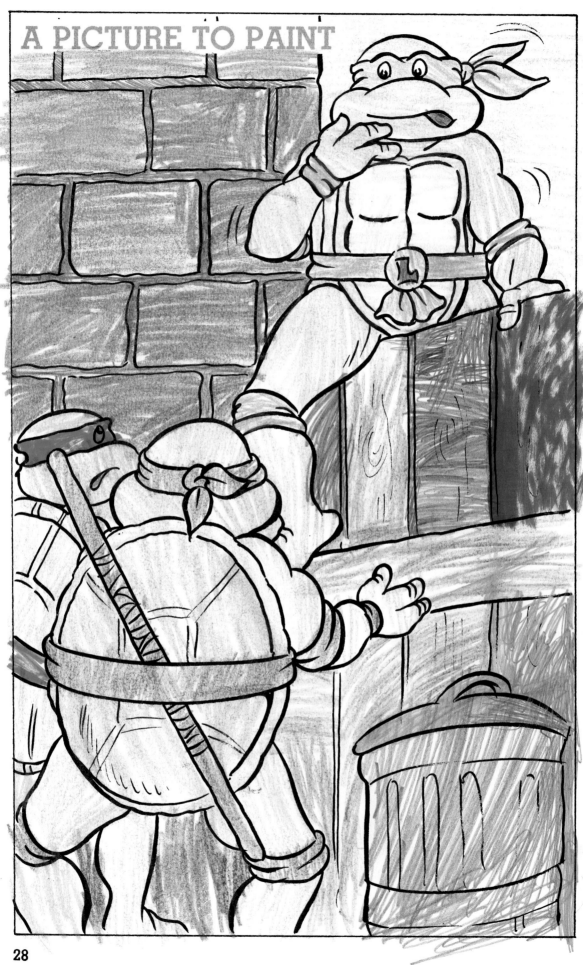

# NEW YORK'S SHINIEST

REACHING HER APARTMENT AFTER WORK ONE DAY, APRIL — WITH HER FRIEND IRMA — FINDS THAT SHE'S IN THE PROCESS OF BEING BURGLED!

HEY! STOP THAT, YOU CREEP!

MAKE ME, LADY!

ONE SIDE! WE GOT WORK TO DO! YUH HUH HUH!

OOH! IF — IF THE *TURTLES* WERE HERE!

S.O.S! COME IN, GUYS!

MOST PEOPLE WOULD CALL THE BOYS IN BLUE — NOT THE BOYS IN GREEN!

FROM THEIR SEWER H.Q., APRIL'S FRIENDS RACE TO THE RESCUE!

HAUL SHELL, DUDES! WE MAY NOT BE IN TIME!

THIS IS IT! LOOK!

YOU GUYS WANNA BUY SOME CHEAP FURNITURE? IT'S A STEAL! YUH YUH!

29

IT'S APRIL'S GEAR. GIVE IT BACK OR ELSE!

ZOWIE! THIS COSTUMED FREAK AND HIS PALS WANT TO *RUMBLE*, FELLERS!

HUP!

GAWSH! THEY'RE TOO STRONG FOR US!

HERE YOU GO, APRIL. ALL WELL AGAIN!

YOU GUYS ARE THE GREATEST THANKS A MILLION!

AND AS FOR THE CRIME IN THIS CITY I'M NOT GONNA BITE IT—

—BUT FIGHT IT! A MAN I KNOW IN THE POLICE OWES ME A FAVOUR...

APRIL—T.V. REPORTER THAT SHE IS—LEARNS OF A SCHEME TO BUILD *ROBOT COPS*. THAT NIGHT.

OOOH. THIS PLACE IS *SCARY!* UH—MISTER..?

IT'S THE PROTOTYPE ROBOT COP!

AND THIS IS HIS CONTROLLER!

HI. I'M REX-1... I AM PROGRAMMED TO OBEY AND PROTECT YOU.

NEATO! WHAT A STORY THIS'LL MAKE!

SHE PHOTOGRAPHS HIM, ASKS QUESTIONS— AND LEAVES. THEN...

KA-RUNNCH!

OOHH!

I SERVE ONLY YOU! I MUST REMAIN WITH YOU!

TO THE SEWERS...

SO YOU SEE, GUYS HE WON'T LEAVE ME!

WHAT ARE YOU GONNA DO WITH SHINY FACE?

I FEAR THIS MEANS TROUBLE...

31

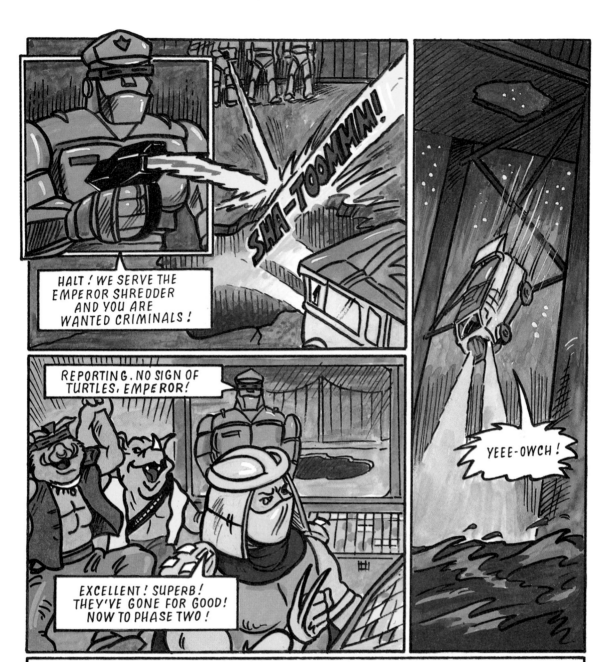

WHILE SPLINTER, APRIL AND REX-1 SET OUT TO TRY AND FIND THE TURTLES!

THERE'S BEEN NO CONTACT. I FEAR THE WORSE.

OH, PLEASE LET THEM BE OKAY!

OH, NO!

SKREE!

LEAVE THIS TO ME.

CUT HIM DOWN!

ONE OF SHREDDER'S ROBOTS FIRES AT MASONRY ABOVE, AND...

DA-RUUMMMBLE

REX ONE!

FEAR NOTHING, APRIL! WE'RE HERE!

YEAH! A DUNKING IN THE RIVER DOESN'T BOTHER US AMPHIBIANS!

LEONARDO FLINGS ONE OF HIS SWORDS. IT CLEAVES POWER LINES, AND BRINGS THEM DOWN!

SHA-ZATTT!

DON'T SWEAT, TURTLES, I'LL HANDLE THIS!

SHA-ZATT! KRAMMMM! FRITTTCH!

WITH THE OPPOSITION OUT OF THE WAY...

CAN YOU MEND HIM, DONATELLO..

YEAH, APRIL, AND RE-PROGRAMME HIM SO THAT HE CONTROLS SHREDDER'S TIN-MEN!

DO YOU HAVE TO USE MY FAVOURITE VIDEO-TAPES?

CERTAINLY I DO, MICHAELANGELO. IT'S IN A GOOD CAUSE!

AND SO, WHEN SHREDDER SENDS IN ALL HIS TROOPS...

RIGHT, YOU GUYS! GET THIS!

ARMS—OUT! LEGS—SPREAD! HUP—TWO—JUMP!

WHAT'S HAPPENED?

MIKE'S AEROBICS TAPE, AND I'VE PROGRAMMED IT TO SPEED UP!

FASTER AND FASTER! UNTIL SHREDDER'S ROBOTS DESTROY THEMSELVES!

SHOOM FLASSH

THAT'S IT, GUYS AND SHREDDER'S GOING TO BE DANCING WITHOUT MY HELP!

WITH RAGE! WELL DONE TURTLES—AND WELL DONE REX-ONE!

# A PICTURE TO PAINT

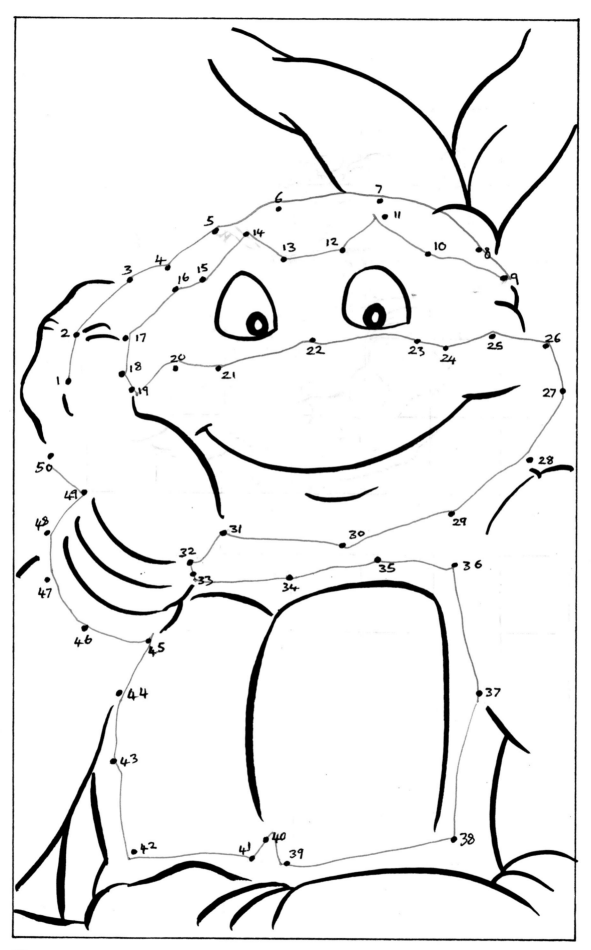

# COPY AND COLOUR

Copy the picture above in the space below using the
grid as a guide. Then colour in both pictures.

SHREDDER

SPLINTER

# WORD SEARCH 2

Can you find the following 15 things associated with
the Turtles in the grid below? They can be spelt backwards,
forwards, up, down or diagonally.
Answers on pages 60-61.

TECHNODROME        SHELLS
DIMENSION X        MUTANTS
NINJA              REPORTER
PIZZA              TELEVISION
NEW YORK           NUNCHAKUS
SEWERS             SAI
SCIENTIST          SWORDS
                   BO

| Z | E | M | O | R | D | O | N | H | C | E | T | D |
|---|---|---|---|---|---|---|---|---|---|---|---|---|
| W | A | U | P | U | B | I | U | V | D | S | I | I |
| S | R | T | A | N | R | W | N | O | E | D | L | M |
| Q | J | A | P | W | E | S | C | E | S | R | F | E |
| T | U | N | T | Q | T | Y | H | A | F | O | V | N |
| S | I | T | R | E | R | H | A | J | K | W | L | S |
| I | N | E | W | Y | O | R | K | A | D | S | A | I |
| T | I | R | E | P | P | O | U | T | G | C | A | O |
| N | N | S | L | L | E | H | S | A | S | T | O | N |
| E | W | U | I | U | R | E | A | Z | J | E | E | X |
| I | G | A | S | I | U | P | V | Z | E | N | S | E |
| C | T | E | L | E | V | I | S | I | O | N | I | B |
| S | E | W | E | R | S | F | M | P | T | H | A | N |

43

# ENTER THE FLY

"Just what do you suppose Shredder's up to *this* time?" Michaelangelo peered down at the rapidly approaching skyline of New York as the Turtle Blimp came cruising in, some five hundred feet above the city.

"You heard April's message," said Leonardo. "He's been spotted on the roof of the World Trade Centre!"

"It's for sure he's not there for the view," chuckled Donatello.

In fact, Shredder - the Turtles' most determined enemy - was conducting an experiment with his ally, the evil scientist, Baxter, to set up some kind of destructive force-field between the twin towers of the huge building. Now, Baxter pushed the commit-button of the machine in front of him. And instead of the unexpected discharge of power, the thing blew up!

"Oh, *no!*" wailed Baxter. "I forgot to reverse the polarity of the neutron flow!"

"You bumbling idiot," raved Shredder. "Why am I condemned to work with *amateurs*?"

At that moment, the arch-criminal caught sight of the blimp from the tail of his eye, and with a series of furious oaths, grabbed up the damaged machine and ran for the roof exit with Baxter hard on his heels.

"Just like that coward to run away," groaned Raphael. "There's no point in giving chase, either. He'll lose us for sure!"

"Looks like the party's over, Dudes," said Michaelangelo. "Let's boogie!"

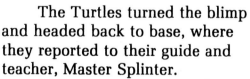

The Turtles turned the blimp and headed back to base, where they reported to their guide and teacher, Master Splinter.

"All we can do is wait for Shredder's next move," mused Splinter.

"Yeah! Wait - and *eat*!" Michaelangelo smacked his lips. "This Turtle is mondo hungry!" He flipped open Splinter's microwave, picked out a pizza, and tossed it into the air, where Leonardo's ninja sword neatly divided it into four equal pieces with a couple of natty swipes. Now there was no sound but steady chomping...

Meanwhile, Shredder and Baxter were out in the middle of the East River on a fly-ridden garbage barge. This was the miserable spot decided upon by Shredder's accomplice, Krang. The sinister Brain-creature from Dimension X. "Sometimes I think Krang has something against me," grumbled Shredder, irritably swiping at the millions of insects buzzing round them.

When Krang appeared on Shredder's hand-held communicator, he was more than angry that the experiment had gone wrong. "You *must* destroy those interfering amphibians before I can begin my master plan to dominate the world," he snarled.

"Then give me more help," snapped Shredder. "Send me Rock Steady and Bebop. Perhaps brawn will succeed where brain has failed!"

Krang agreed. He was sick of the presence of Rock Steady and Bebop in Dimension X, in any case. Shredder's two enormous musclemen, as thick in the head as deep-pile carpets, were enough to make anyone long for peace and quiet. "But," said Krang, "the inter-dimensional energy balance is very fragile at the moment. I must have someone sent back here in exchange."

"No problem," sneered Shredder. And without more ado, he picked up Baxter and hurled the squealing scientist through the strange, multi-coloured cloud that was the portal between the normal world and Dimension X.

Even as Baxter vanished, Rock Steady and Bebop came hurtling down in return, the pair of them landing head-first in the foul-smelling garbage.

"Gee, thanks, boss," said Bebop, picking himself out. "But we'd *already* eaten."

"Silence, you fool," barked Shredder. "You're here to help me settle with the Turtles, once and for all!"

"Great!" laughed Rock Steady. "Consider them, like, history! Where do we start?"

Shredder rubbed his hands. "First, we strike at their weakest point. April O'Neill!"

The beautiful Channel Six Television reporter was busy at her office computer when a special messenger arrived, carrying a strange and lovely pot plant. "For you," he said. There was no card with the gift, and he had gone before April could ask who'd sent it. Little did she realise that it had come directly from Shredder!

Instead, she assumed that the Turtles had sent it, and she was just a little annoyed. "They shouldn't give me flowers," she said. "After all, there's nothing *romantic* between us!"

Right away, she made tracks for the Turtles' headquarters to return the present, but there, she found only Master Splinter.

"What the..?" Splinter's eye fell on the plant, and he snatched it from her hands, hurling it into a dustbin. "That's the sinister Doku Plant," he gasped. "You - you didn't breathe in any of the perfume..?"

"Well, yes...I did.." began April. But then, suddenly, she began to feel faint, and within seconds, she had keeled over, totally unconscious!

At the same time, in the Technodrome - Krang's headquarters - Krang had taken a dislike to the scientist, Baxter. On a whim, he had his slave robots toss the unfortunate man into the big disintegrator chamber.

Baxter's cries mingled with the frantic buzzing of a fly that had accidentally flown in there with him. But suddenly, startlingly, the totally unexpected happened! Instead of disintegrating, scientist and fly became as one - and when the door of the chamber opened, it was human insect that came buzzing out! Baxter and the fly had cross-mutated.

"Treat meee as an innnnsect, would they?" Baxter's buzzing voice shrilled out as he smashed a panel and seized a ray-gun. He flew straight for the controls of the inter-dimensional transfer machine, and punched the buttons. Three slave robots almost got to him, but he turned and blasted them before he took off and disappeared back into the normal world.

The Turtles returned to Master Splinter to discover that their friend, April, lay in deadly danger! "Can't you *do* something, master?" asked Leonardo.

"I can make up an antidote," said Splinter. "But only if I can get hold of the leaves of a Gazai Plant - and as far as I know there are none in this part of the world!"

"There's that weird garden centre just out of town," muttered Donatello. "If anyone has a Gazai Plant, it'll be them!"

"So what are we *waiting* for?" roared Michaelangelo. "C'mon! Let's haul shell!"

The Turtles got lucky. There was *one* Gazai Plant. The very last in the Western Hemisphere. They paid up, grabbed it, and took off. But *that* was when Baxter buzzed in!

"I ssseek revennnnge," he zizzed. "On all my enemies! And there - *there* are the Turrrrtlessss!"

Ray-gun blasting, Baxter came zooming out of the sky - and wild shots fanned the sidewalk around Leonardo and his pals! In the nick of time, Donatello found a dustbin, yanked off the shiny metal lid, and diverted a lancing blast of power. A second later and he'd have been fried! Raphael had to use all his skills to dance and dodge Baxter's but it was Leonardo who temporarily put paid to the cross-mutant's attack. Whirling his ninja sword into the air, he severed a line of washing hanging from a tenement front, and the clothes fell, to drape themselves around Baxter, preventing him from shooting with any accuracy.

The four Turtles made good their escape, diving down a manhole cover and slamming it behind them even as Baxter recovered his aim. They heard the shots spanging off the cover as they raced headlong for safety down the long tunnel of a storm-drain sewer.

Furious at losing his prey, Baxter set his mind on another target. Shredder! He found him plotting with Rock Steady and Bebop, and went straight in, his ray-

gun blasting. But he was no match for the two strong-arm thugs, who shot him down.

"Why were you shooting at me?" roared Shredder. "Do you think I am your enemy?"

"Yessss," hissed Baxter - but Shredder's hypnotic eyes bored into his, and the cross-mutant fell silent. "It's the *Turtles* who sent you back to Dimension X," rasped Shredder. "Don't you remember..? Krang told me of the - er - unfortunate accident that turned you into a human fly. But it was the *Turtles'* fault!"

Baxter believed Shredder's lies, and now he swore vengeance again on the hard-shell heroes. "Fear nothing, master," he spat. "I will ffffffind them! And whennn I *doooo...*"

Time was running out for April, lying in an ever-deepening coma while Master Splinter paced up and down, up and down...But time also seemed to be running out for the Turtles! With the super-power of his multiple-lensed fly-eyes, Baxter spotted them come out of the sewer, and immediately contacted Shredder. "I've ffffound them, massster!"

"Good," said Shredder, who was busy testing one of Baxter's last devices - a kind of mechanical spider which pounced on its victims and wrapped them tightly in unbreakable rope. "Where are they?"

"Well," said Baxter, "I'm not exxxactly ssssure. But there's a nice pizza parlour on the corrrrner!"

"That narrows it down," said Shredder sarcastically. "You *bughead.* Just wait until I get a fix on your transmission. Stay with them. I shall be there!"

"What - uh - about *us,* boss?" Bebop was standing with his thumb in his mouth, looking at Rock Steady. And Rock Steady? He was upside down, suspended in the air by a wrapping of rope from the spider machine. "Ah. Hmmm." Shredder rubbed his hands. "I see the thing works. You've given it a good test, Rock Steady."

"Gee! I ain't never *passed* a test in my life," said Rock Steady. "An' here I am, actually *givin'* 'em! Like wow!" He added: "Can I get loose now, boss?"

Shredder set him free. "I shall call this machine after you," he chuckled. "I shall call it - 'Knucklehead'."

"Wowie! *Thanks,* boss!"

By this time, of course, Baxter had got tired of just buzzing around. Besides, the Turtles weren't in the mood for standing still. So, Baxter checked out his ray-gun and, once more, went in to the attack!

As shots beat up the roadway, the Turtles groaned. "It's that fly again!"

"Head for the blimp," yelled Donatello. "Quick - follow me!"

Suddenly, a big van cut across their path and blocked the street crossing. "Isn't that typical?" said Michaelangelo. "Whenever you need a traffic warden, he ain't there!" He shouted at the van. "Hey, buddy! Don't you know that pedestrians have the right of way?"

The side door flew open, and there stood Shredder. "Pedestrians, yes. Amphibians, no!" he roared. He whipped out a ray device like a camera, and a huge blast of power sent the Turtles reeling! But Donatello was on balance within a split second, and he pole-vaulted himself forward with his long staff to plant his feet squarely in Shredder's chest and send the villain spinning. "The stick is mightier than the blaster," he crowed.

On his knees, Shredder punched out a call-sign on a control box, and the spider machine - 'The Knucklehead' - came out to fling itself at Donatello. "Ready for another surprise?" Shredder scrambled to his feet and waved his arm. Instantly, Rock Steady and Bebop appeared from the van and rushed the other three Turtles!

"Ready to shoot an' loot!" bellowed Bebop. "Say goodbye, Turtles!" But even as he and his sidekick fired, Leonardo sprang forward, both ninja swords leaping into his hands. The glittering blades neatly deflected the thugs' fire, and the twin blasts of power hit 'The Knucklehead'! Instantly, the weird spider-machine coughed, kicked, jumped in the air and fell on its back, Donatello tumbling clear!

"Why, you cretins!" roared Shredder. "Now look what you've done!"

"Duhhh - *we* didn't know he was gonna do that," whimpered Bebop.

"We don't even know what 'cretins' means," added Rock Steady. Away and running, the Turtles made for the blimp, and took off. But Baxter was hard on their heels, and even though the heroes gained height, he was able to follow. His ray-gun blasted the link between the driving pod and the blimp's gasbag, and next instant, the four friends were planing down to one heck of a shell-jarring landing in the streets below.

A screech of brakes, and the enemy van was blocking their path again. "Now, Turtles," snarled Shredder. "This is for keeps!"

"We can't have a battle *here*," said Leonardo. "Look at those buildings. They're a national monument!"

"Shredder is a vandal," snapped Donatello. "He'd trash *anything!*"

"I have an idea," said Michaelangelo. "C'mon, Dudes - we can get back to the blimp *my* way!"

The four of them scaled the facade of the nearest building, heaving themselves up a tall tower, ignoring bravely the battering of ray-gun fire that surrounded them as they climbed. They reached the roof...swarmed, one by one, up the flagpole on top, and jumped together for the dangling ropes of the blimp as it sailed past.

The escape took them away from the action - but they couldn't hold on for long. "Turtle-Trooper Chute Packs," yelled Leonardo, and they fell away before parachutes opened to drift them to safety...

There was only one problem. A real biggy. In all the excitement, the vital Gazai Plant had been dropped - and Baxter had grabbed it!

It was four glum Turtles who reported to Master Splinter that, although they'd escaped Shredder and his goons, they'd lost the Gazai.

"You must get it back," muttered Splinter. He gestured to the stricken girl. "Without it, April will die. And time is running out. Fast!"

"We'll find Shredder if we have to crumble the city and sift the bits," said Leonardo. But at that moment, the communicator in Splinter's room came to life, and Shredder himself appeared on it. "I patched into your network," he snarled. "And I have an invitation for the Turtles."

"We ain't in the mood to party, Dude," said Michaelangelo. "Unless," he added, "you get some pizza, maybe..?"

"I challenge you," said Shredder, ignoring the wisecrack, "to a straight fight. Four to four. You against me and my team. If you win - you get the Gazai Plant!"

"He's challenging us to a fair fight?" Donatello gasped. "He can't even *spell* 'fair'. I'm amazed he can *pronounce* it!"

"We have no choice, though," said Raphael. "Come on, guys. Let's get movin'..."

Sure enough, it was a trap. Shredder had chosen a vast junkyard for the battle, and Baxter had hastily fixed up a pair of concealed electrodes on both sides of a path between some ruined cars. "These will ssshift the microcellular structure forward in time. It will mean that they become out of phase with the living world. In sssshort - they will dissssappear. *For everrr!*"

"Heh, heh, heh," gloated Shredder. "Then we must be sure to drive those confounded Turtles between the electrodes. They will suspect nothing!"

"A nice place Shredder picked," said Leonardo as they arrived. "A scrapyard. Kind of fits his personality."

"Exactomundo," said Michaelangelo. "Say - where *is* old tin-skin. anyway?"

"Right here, Turtles!" Shredder stepped out behind them. He held up the Gazai Plant. "Come and get it - or, are you - *afraid*?"

"*Us*? *Afraid*? *Never*!" chorused the Turtles - but at that instant, Bebop and Rock Steady broke from cover and began blasting at them - while Baxter spun out from above and set the ground leaping with a series of bracketing shots.

"I hate to say this - but *fall back*!" Leonardo was totally unaware that he was retreating straight towards the deadly electrodes. *Just* as Shredder had planned.

They were within a hair's-breadth of passing between them when - right out of the blue - a cascade of falling car bodies heralded the smash-through arrival of none other than Master Splinter, at the wheel of the Turtle-Mobile. Fire from the roof cannons disarmed the thugs, and blew the vital Gazai Plant straight into Donatello's hands. "Get it *back*!" screamed Shredder to Baxter - but the cross-mutant was over eager. His flight took him straight between the electrodes, and in a blinding flash of light, he vanished for ever.

Outclassed and bewildered, Shredder and his two heavies quit the scene. They'd played their hand - and lost!

"Not bad shooting, Splinter," mused Leonardo. "For someone who doesn't believe in violence!" Master Splinter blushed. "It was not violence against the *person*," he said. "And *that* is what matters."

Back at headquarters, Splinter mixed up the antidote from the leaves of the Gazai Plant, and the Turtles raised a cheer as April's eyes fluttered open. "Wh - where *am* I..? Oh, hi, guys..?"

Moments later, a strange perfume began to drift through the room. Leonardo gulped. "Oh - oh! I hope that's not another of those deadly Doku Plants!"

"Nope," beamed Michaelangelo, coming in from the kitchen. "It's another pizza I just invented. Anchovies smothered in spare Gazai."

"Yukkkk!" came the chorus.

"I was hopin' you'd say that, Dudes," laughed Michaelangelo. "Means all the more for me! Here's Gazai in your eye!" he started stuffing his face...

BEBOP + ROCKSTEADY

# SPOT THE DIFFERENCE

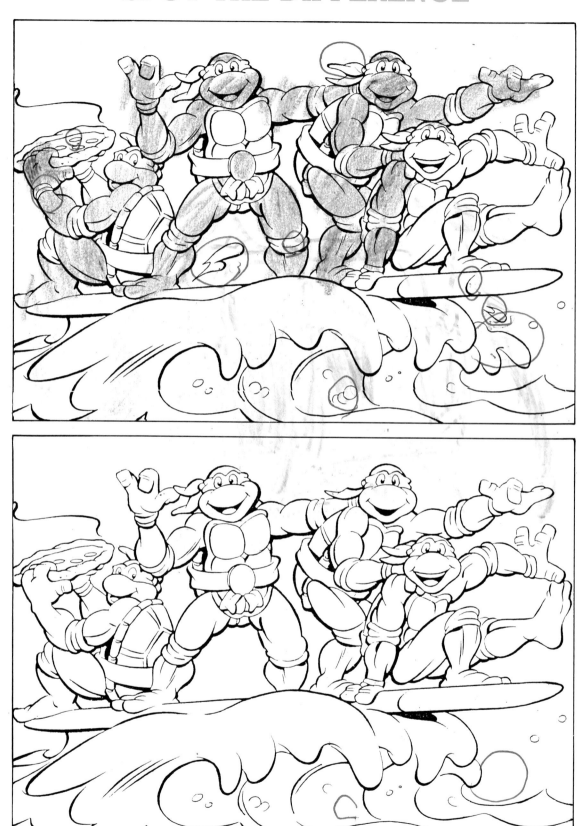

There are 10 differences between the pictures above!
How many can you spot? Answers on pages 60-61.

# ANSWERS

## SPOT THE DIFFERENCE

## WORD SEARCH 1

## WORD SEARCH 2

| | | | | | | | | | | | | |
|---|---|---|---|---|---|---|---|---|---|---|---|---|
| Z | E | M | O | R | D | O | N | H | C | E | T | D |
| W | A | U | P | U | B | I | U | V | D | S | I | I |
| S | R | T | A | N | R | W | N | O | E | D | L | M |
| Q | J | A | P | W | E | S | C | E | S | R | F | E |
| T | U | N | T | Q | T | Y | H | A | F | O | V | N |
| S | I | T | R | E | R | H | A | J | K | W | L | S |
| N | E | W | Y | O | R | K | A | D | T | A | T | T |
| T | I | R | E | P | P | O | U | T | G | C | A | O |
| N | N | S | L | L | E | H | S | A | S | T | O | N |
| E | W | U | I | U | R | E | A | Z | E | E | K | K |
| | G | A | S | I | U | P | V | Z | E | N | S | E |
| C | T | E | L | E | V | I | S | I | O | N | I | B |
| S | E | W | E | R | S | F | M | P | T | H | A | N |

## SPOT THE DIFFERENCE

PRINTED IN BELGIUM BY
INTERNATIONAL BOOK PRODUCTION

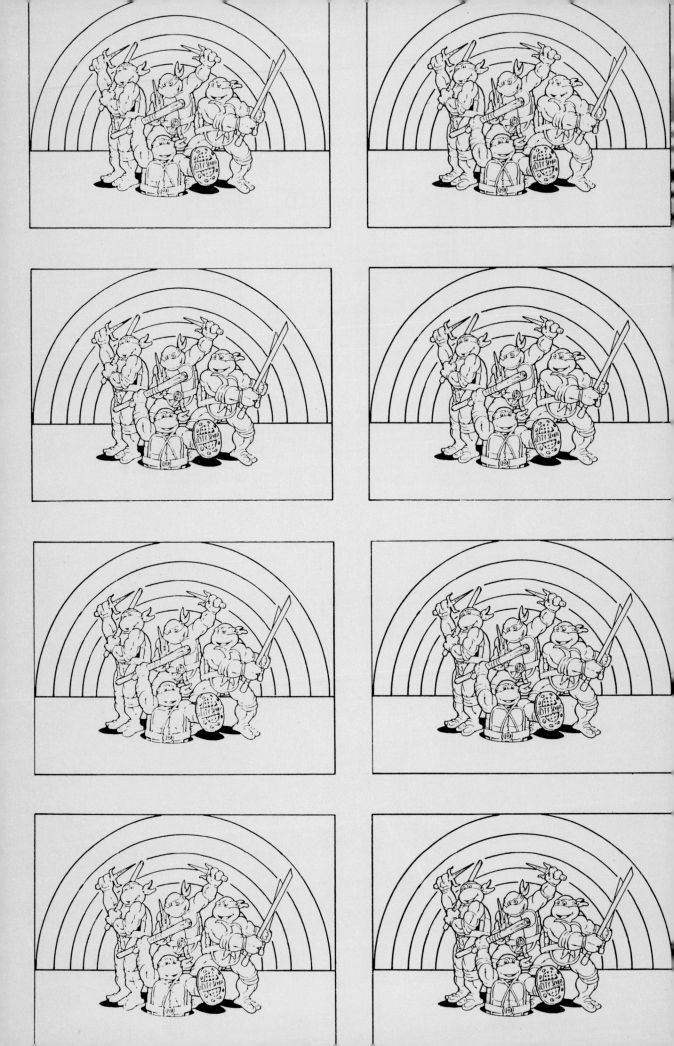